ONCE UPON A TIME...

...On the faraway world of Eternia, twins were born to the king and queen. But soon after their birth, the little brother and sister were separated by fate.

The boy, Prince Adam, grew up on the planet Eternia. There, he learned the secrets of Castle Grayskull and that he had a great destiny. Through a magical transformation, he became He-Man, the most powerful man in the universe, and he fought on the side of goodness.

His sister, Princess Adora, was kidnapped as a baby by the wicked Hordak. She was raised by him on the planet Etheria, a world that lived in misery under the rule of Hordak and his Horde.

Only after many years were Prince Adam and Princess Adora reunited. Like Prince Adam, Adora was given a magical weapon; hers was called the Sword of Protection. Adora's Sword of Protection gave her mighty powers. With it, she was transformed into She-Ra, the Princess of Power. Her beautiful horse Spirit became Swift Wind, a flying unicorn.

Adora stayed on Etheria to work on the side of the Rebellion, which was determined to return freedom to the land. This small but dedicated band was led by Angella, queen of the Kingdom of Bright Moon.

Adora guarded the secret of She-Ra carefully. Of her many friends, only the centuries-old Madame Razz and little Kowl knew who She-Ra, the Princess of Power, really was.

One other possessed the secret of She-Ra. High atop a mountain was the Crystal Castle, a shining palace that was She-Ra's special place. At the bottom of a mysterious pool in the castle dwelled the spirit of Light Hope, She-Ra's powerful friend.

No one but She-Ra could see this wonderful castle. And only on the day that all Etheria was free would Light Hope's secrets be known to all.

It was for that day, when goodness would reign again over Etheria, that She-Ra pledged her power.

The Queen of the Ball

Written by Bryce Knorr

Illustrated by Harry J. Quinn and James Holloway

Creative Direction by Jacquelyn A. Lloyd

Design Direction by Ralph E. Eckerstrom

A GOLDEN BOOK

Western Publishing Company, Inc.
Racine, Wisconsin 53404

Library of Congress Catalog Card Number 84-062813
ISBN 0-932631-07-X
A B C D E F G H I J

Classic™ Binding U.S. Patent #4,408,780
Patented in Canada 1984.
Patents in other countries issued or pending.
R. R. Donnelley and Sons Company

"Come on, Spirit," said the little Twigget Pluck. "Don't eat all the flowers. Leave some for me to put in Adora's hair."

"Oh, to be a girl again," Madame Razz sighed. "I loved putting flowers in my hair when I was young."

Adora and Glimmer tried not to laugh. Razz was a thousand years old, more or less.

"Etheria was so nice in the old days," Razz sighed. "The Horde didn't tell us what to do. We only worried about what to wear to the ball. We had such beautiful dances."

"That sounds great!" Glimmer said.

"It must have been fun," Adora added. "I wish we could go to a ball."

Glimmer's eyes lit up. She touched the jewel in her staff. She flashed across the clearing on a beam of light.

"Why don't *we* have a ball?" she asked. "My mother is the queen, after all. We could wear beautiful dresses."

A lovely gown made of light appeared on Glimmer.

"Everyone would dance with me, of course," she said. "*I* am the princess of Bright Moon."

Adora sighed. She was a princess, too. The Princess of Power. "But I cannot tell my friends about She-Ra's secrets," she thought.

"Will you teach me to dance, Madame Razz?" Adora asked. "I'm afraid I can't dance as well as I'd like to. When I was with Hordak, he never used to let me have any fun."

"Tut, tut, my dear," Madame Razz said. She grabbed Broom, who was sleeping against a tree. "There is nothing to it. Anyone can dance. And you have a natural grace. Almost as if *you* were a princess." Madame Razz winked at Adora and whispered, "And we both know that you truly *are* a real princess."

"Just close your eyes," Razz continued out loud. "Pretend you are as light as a feather. You will float away!"

Razz and Broom spun 'round and 'round. Faster and faster they went. They took off into the air!

"Goodbye, girls," Razz waved. "It looks like we are going somewhere!"

"We should go, too," Adora said.

She whistled and Spirit came trotting to her side. Pluck took a flower hanging from the horse's mouth. He put it in Adora's hair.

"There!" the Twigget said. "Your hair is done. You look like a princess now."

"Thank you, Pluck," Adora said. "I feel like one, too."

They left for Castle Bright Moon. All Glimmer could talk about was the ball. She flashed here and there, talking to a "prince."

"Why thank you, sir prince," Glimmer pretended. "I would love to dance."

Glimmer's act made Adora laugh.

"Will I ever dance with a prince?" she asked herself.

When they got home, Queen Angella read them a letter. "It's from Prince Defiant," she said. "He's coming to visit us. He may join our Rebellion."

"A real prince!" Glimmer said excitedly. "Oh Mother, I have a great idea. Let's have a ball!"

"This is serious, Glimmer," the queen told her daughter. "Dancing won't help us beat The Horde. Besides, no one has had a ball for years."

"Glimmer does have a good idea," Adora said. "A ball might get Prince Defiant on our side."

"Well . . ." Queen Angella said. "Maybe you are right. Prince Defiant could choose the queen of the ball. She would be the fairest girl in the kingdom.

"If only I had my crown. I could wear it to the dance. But Catra took it."

The missing crown gave Adora an idea.

"I must get Angella's crown back," Adora thought. "We need its magical power. Maybe I can teach Catra a lesson, too."

Adora went to get Spirit. She raised her Sword of Protection.
"By the honor of Grayskull," she said.

"I AM SHE-RA!"

Into the night, She-Ra, the Princess of Power, flew on Swift Wind. Near the edge of the Fright Zone, they landed. Only one other person knew about this secret place.

The winged unicorn neighed three times. A bird sang back three times.

She-Ra gave the password. Double Trouble stepped out from the shadows. "I got your message," She-Ra's secret agent said. "I came quickly."

"We have an important job for you," She-Ra said. "But you can't tell anyone. Not even Angella. This must be a secret.

"Tell Catra about the ball. I must get her away from her tower."

The day of the ball was near. Everyone in the kingdom of Bright Moon was excited.

"No one knows what Prince Defiant looks like," Glimmer said. "But he must be very handsome."

Glimmer tried on dress after dress. She wanted to be queen of the ball.

"Being a princess is such hard work!" Glimmer said, sinking down onto her bed. "My staff is drained. And so am I! I must take a nap."

But Adora did not have time to rest. She went to the ballroom.

"My plan to get back Angella's crown is set," she thought. "Catra will come to the ball. I know she will want to be queen. When she is here, I'll go to her tower and get the crown."

Adora thought she was alone. "I must make sure I can dance like a princess," she said. "It's time to practice."

Adora began to dance.

"You dance just like a princess," Madame Razz said. She stepped from the shadows into the light.

"I do?" Adora asked. "Oh, Razz. You know I'm a princess. But no one else does. I hope I can dance like a princess at the ball."

"You will do just fine," Razz said. "A princess must believe in herself. So here's a spell to help you:

"When the prince takes your hand,

"You will dance simply grand."

Everyone was ready on the day of the ball. And that included Catra. "Won't Angella be surprised to see me," Catra said. "I will be the queen of her ball. I have made sure of that. I will be the queen of Bright Moon, too. This is the last dance for Angella, Adora and the Rebellion!"

Catra changed into her cat disguise. She put Angella's crown in her cape and turned to the Twigget Pluck. He was very scared.

"Now, my little Twigget," she said. "Show us the way to Castle Bright Moon. That's why we caught you. Get going!"

Magicat took a few steps, then stopped. His tracks glowed in the dark. "The spell works!" Catra said. "My army will follow our tracks to Angella's castle."

Prince Defiant was ready for the dance, too. But Glimmer was disappointed.

"He does not look like a prince," she told Adora.

"He does not act like one, either," said Adora. "He's very spoiled."

"But he's the only prince here," Glimmer said. "I have to dance with him."

Finally, the music began. Adora stayed near the door. She was ready to slip away and begin her secret mission.

"May I have this dance, Adora?" Bow asked. He took Adora to the dance floor. But the prince tapped him on the shoulder.

"I'm cutting in," the prince said.

Adora saw her chance to get away.

"Go right ahead, prince," Adora said. She left Bow and the prince together. "But you may look funny dancing with Bow."

Prince Defiant was angry. But he rushed after Adora.

"You *must* dance with me," he said. "I am choosing the queen of the ball."

"Here goes," Adora thought. She remembered Madame Razz' spell. "I can dance like a princess. When the prince takes my hand, I will dance just grand."

But it was the prince who couldn't dance. He tripped Adora, and she stumbled.

"Razz must have got it wrong," Adora thought. "When he tries to dance, I don't have a chance.

"But this may be just what I need."

"Ouch," Adora said. "I hurt my ankle."

Prince Defiant didn't care. "My goodness," he said. "You can't dance. You will never be the queen of the ball."

Bow and Kowl helped Adora up. "Who does he think he is?" Bow asked. His heart was pounding very hard. This was his special warning of danger. "I'd like to make him sing a different tune."

"Thank you, Bow and Kowl," Adora said. "You both are gentlemen. I'm going to lie down for a while."

"You will be back, won't you?" Bow asked. "You should be here for the naming of the queen."

"I'll be back," Adora said. She left, but not for her room.

Adora went to get Spirit. She made sure they were alone. "By the honor of Grayskull," she said, raising her Sword of Protection.

"I AM SHE-RA!"

"I have a feeling you want to go somewhere fast," Swift Wind said. The unicorn flew to her side. "Where to?"

"To the Fright Zone," She-Ra said. "We have a crown to get back."

When they reached Catra's tower, She-Ra was careful. "I don't see anyone," she said.

"Is it a trap?" Swift Wind asked.

"I don't know," She-Ra answered. "I can feel someone in trouble. He's up in Catra's tower. Come on!"

Swift Wind flew up to a tower window. She-Ra took careful aim and jumped. Through the window, she saw that a man was tied up.

She pulled herself through the window and took off the man's ropes. "You...you are a girl," he said.

"That's right," she said. "I am She-Ra, the Princess of Power. But who are you? And what are you doing at Catra's?"

"Prince Defiant, at your service," he bowed. "Catra found out I was coming to Angella's ball. She sent a guard in my place. The fake prince will make her the queen of the ball.

"And that's not all. Her army is following her. She has Angella's crown. Catra wants to take over the castle!"

"We must get you to the ball and stop Catra," She-Ra said. She heard a whistle outside. It was Double Trouble.

"I'm glad I found you," Double Trouble said. "Catra thinks her army is following her. But she's in for a surprise..."

Back at Castle Bright Moon, the band suddenly stopped. Catra rode into the ball on Magicat. No one said a word.

"I don't want trouble," Catra lied. "I only want a chance to be the queen of the ball."

"We can't trust her," Bow said. His heart began to pound even harder than before.

"She should have a chance," the fake Prince Defiant said. "I won't name a queen if Catra can't stay."

Angella let the prince have his way. She still wanted him to join the Rebellion.

"Catra will have a chance," the queen said. "Let the ball continue."

The fake prince jumped onto the stage.

"I have made up my mind," he shouted. "Catra is the queen of the ball!"

"No!" everyone yelled. But Catra went up to the stage. She took Angella's crown from her cape.

"I am not only queen of the ball," she said. "I am the queen of Bright Moon. My army is outside. Your kingdom is mine!"

"Sorry to disappoint you, Catra," She-Ra said from the doorway.

She and the real prince rode into the ballroom on Swift Wind.

"Our friends changed Magicat's tracks," She-Ra said. "Your army is lost."
Swift Wind flew toward the stage. The real Prince Defiant grabbed the
crown from Catra. She-Ra swung at a rope with her Sword of Protection.
Hundreds of balloons fell from the ceiling. Catra was covered with them.

The rebels grabbed Catra. "What should we do with her?" Bow asked. "I know how to punish Catra," Prince Defiant said. "Let her see me name the real queen of the ball."

The prince looked for She-Ra. But she was gone. Then he remembered Angella's crown.

"There is only one queen in Bright Moon," the prince said. He put the crown on Angella's head. Everyone cheered.

"Your cause is just," he said. "I will join your Rebellion."

"You won this time," Catra said. "But She-Ra will not beat me again!"

Catra jumped on Magicat. They ran from the ballroom. The fake prince ran after her, chased by loud boos from the crowd.

"There is time for one more dance," Angella said. "With whom will you dance, Prince Defiant?"

   Madame Razz pushed a shy and beautiful Adora forward from the back of the ballroom.
   "This is Adora," Razz said. "She has never danced with a prince."
   "I am honored," the prince said.
   "I *can* dance like a princess," Adora thought. Soon she felt as light as a feather.
   "Why, you're lovely, and you dance just like a princess," Prince Defiant

said. "That is something Catra will never be. Catra is pretty. But her beauty is only skin-deep."

Adora agreed. "How a person looks doesn't matter. A really beautiful person has kindness and love on the inside."

"I met someone like that tonight. Her name is She-Ra, the Princess of Power," Defiant said. "I wonder if she could dance as well as you can?"

Adora just smiled.

THE END